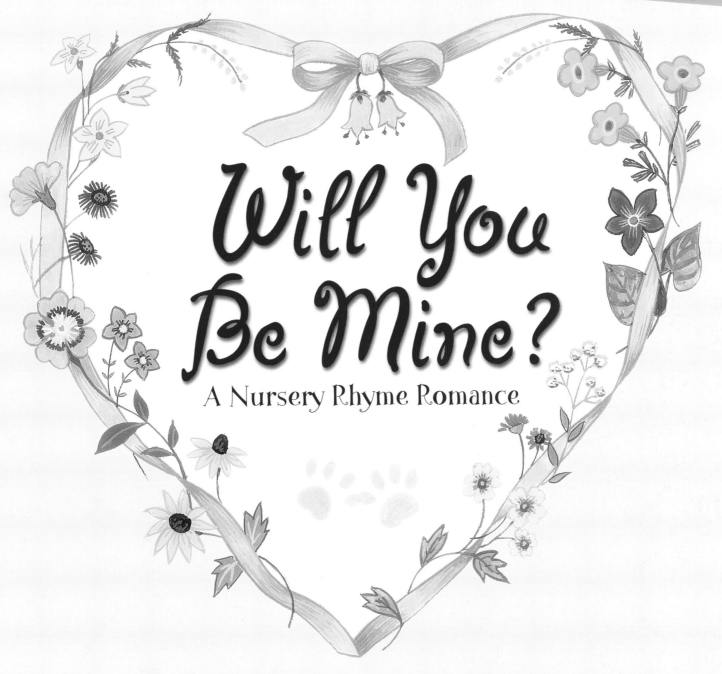

Will You Be Mine?

A Nursery Rhyme Romance

Compiled and illustrated by

Phyllis Limbacher Tildes

Charlesbridge

I dedicate this unique collection of old English nursery rhymes
to my mother, and to the generations of mothers who have
delighted little minds with such sing-song silliness. There are many
variations on traditional Mother Goose tales and nursery rhymes.
For this collection, I strung together some well-loved favorites
and some less familiar rhymes to create an original love story.

—P. L. T.

Published by Charlesbridge
85 Main Street
Watertown, MA 02472
(617) 926-0329
www.charlesbridge.com

Library of Congress Cataloging-in-Publication Data
Tildes, Phyllis Limbacher.
    Will you be mine? : a nursery rhyme romance / Phyllis Limbacher Tildes.
        p. cm.
    Summary: Pretty lasses meet bonnie lads in this illustrated collection of
classic nursery rhymes.
    ISBN 978-1-58089-244-5 (reinforced for library use)
    ISBN 978-1-58089-245-2 (softcover)
1. Nursery rhymes. 2. Children's poetry. [1. Nursery rhymes.] I. Mother
Goose. II. Title.
PZ8.3.T454Wi 2011
398.8—dc22   2010007590

Printed in Singapore
(hc) 10 9 8 7 6 5 4 3 2 1
(sc) 10 9 8 7 6 5 4 3 2 1

Illustrations done in gouache on 4-ply Strathmore Bristol 500 paper
Display type and text type set in Cafe Mimi and Violastix
Color separations by Chroma Graphics, Singapore
Printed and bound September 2010 by Imago in Singapore
Production supervision by Brian G. Walker
Designed by Diane M. Earley

Hickory, dickory dock,
The mouse ran up the clock.
The clock struck one,
The mouse ran down.
Hickory, dickory dock.

The cock's on the housetop blowing his horn;
The bull's in the barn threshing the corn;
The maids in the meadows are gathering hay;
The ducks in the river are swimming away.

A pretty little girl in a round-eared cap,
I met in the lane t'other day;
She gave me such a thump,
That my heart went bump;
I thought I should have fainted away!

Willy boy, Willy boy, where are you going?
I will go with you if I may.

I'm going to the meadow to see them a'mowing,
I'm going to help them make hay.

Birds of a feather will flock together,

And so will pigs and swine;

Rats and mice
will have their choice,

And so will I have mine.

Bonnie lass, pretty lass, will you be mine?
You shall not wash dishes,
Nor feed the swine.
You shall sit on a cushion, and sew a fine seam,
And you shall eat strawberries, sugar, and cream!

Hoddley, poddley, puddles and fogs,
Cats are to marry poodle dogs;
Cats in blue jackets and dogs in red hats,
What will become of the mice and the rats?

Guest List
Polly Flinders
Tom Tucker
Bo Peep
Simple S
Jack S
and
Hump
Pete
Ja
O

Higglety, pigglety, pop!
The dog has eaten the mop;
The pig's in a hurry,
The cat's in a flurry,
Higglety, pigglety, pop!

This little piggy went to market;

This little piggy stayed home;

This little piggy ate roast beef;

This little piggy had none;

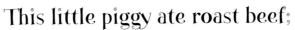

And this little piggy went wee, wee, wee, All the way home.

Pretty John Watts,
We are troubled with rats;
Will you drive them out of the house?
We have mice too in plenty,
That feast in the pantry,
But let them stay,
And nibble away;
What harm is a little brown mouse?

Six little mice sat down to spin;
Pussy passed by and she peeped in.
What are you doing, my little men?
Weaving coats for gentlemen.
Shall I come in and cut off your threads?
No, no, Mistress Pussy, you'd bite off our heads.
Oh, no, I'll not; I'll help you spin.
That may be so, but you don't come in.

On Saturday night shall be my care
To powder my locks and curl my hair . . .

... On Sunday morning my love will come in,
When he shall marry me with a gold ring.

Ride a cock-horse
 To Banbury Cross,
To see a fine lady
 Upon a white horse,
With rings on her fingers,
 And bells on her toes,
And she shall have music
 Wherever she goes.

Banbury Cross
FAIR GROUNDS

Wedding Reception Today!

I danced with the girl
With a hole in her stocking,
And her heel kept a-rocking,
And her heel kept a-rocking,

I danced with the girl
With a hole in her stocking,
We danced by the light of the moon.

The moon shines bright,
The stars give light,
And you may kiss
A pretty girl
At ten o'clock at night.

Bell-horses, bell-horses,
What time of day?
One o'clock, two o'clock,
Off and away!

Pussycat, pussycat, where have you been?
I've been to London to visit the Queen.
Pussycat, pussycat, what did you there?
I frightened a little mouse under her chair.

There was an old crow
Sat upon a clod;
That's the end of my song—
That's odd.

$7.95

Hoddley, poddley, puddles and fogs,
Cats are to marry poodle dogs!

A dapper cat and a demure dog find love and
happiness in this charming collection of
Mother Goose rhymes. With nursery rhymes
both familiar and new, *Will You Be Mine?*
is the perfect choice for your Valentine.

ISBN 978-1-58089-245-2

50795

9 781580 892452

SATURDAY SANCOCHO

Leyla Torres

DIVERSIFY YOUR BOOKSHELF